For Abby and Zack - Such an honor to be your dad!

Acknowledgements

A BIG thanks to Mrs. Savory's 2nd graders, for your
editing expertise and your star-wish-star sandwiches!
Annika (with 2 n's), Carson, Celeste, Eduardo, Ellie,
Ella, Emma, Eunice, Frankie, Hannah, Hunter, Jayden,
Joey, José, Kai, Kenny, Lilly, Marley, MJ, Owen, Ryder,
Spencer, Willow, Zack, & Zoey

Text copyright © 2013 by Derek Munson
Illustrations copyright © 2013 by Derek Munson

Book Design by Melody Wang
Typeset in New Century Schoolbook
Ilustrations were rendered with pencil and watercolor

ISBN-10: 0-9898-4883-3
ISBN-13: 978-0-9898-4883-1

Printed in China
10 9 8 7 6 5 4 3 2 1

Cannonball Books LLC
www.cannonballbooks.com

Bad Dad

By
Derek Munson

Illustrated by
Melody Wang

Cannonball Books

Dad broke the bed.
Bad Dad.

He ate the last cookie from the cookie jar, and drank milk straight out of the carton! Bad Dad.

He helped too much at the science fair.

And guess who got us all in trouble in the toy section at the Shop and Spend? Yep. Bad Dad!

The dentist told him we weren't flossing enough.

The library called. Our books are overdue. By a month.

And he really needs to fix that hole in the fence.

He played ball in the house.
Dad bad! Mom mad.

He stayed up too late playing video games. Again.

The next morning, *we* had to
wake *him* up and we were late
for school. Again.

Another dollar in the sorry jar.

Oh, Dad. That's bad!

Mom was right. He never should have let
us watch that scary movie.

And he's not allowed to cut our hair ever again.
Very, very bad.

Sometimes we think Dad gets in
trouble more than we do!

But he's not all bad ...

He works on my bike,
and helps out with our
homework.

He lets us keep our rooms just the way we like them.

He tells lots of jokes. Sometimes, they're even funny!

He knows tons of games, and sometimes he even wins.

And even though he's big, he always finds
the best places to hide.

He didn't want a hamster, but
we got one.

The drum sets were loud, but he bought one.

He was terrified of grizzly bears, but he fought one.

Just kidding. But I bet he would.

He banished Brussels sprouts from our house forever.

We always love it when he
tries to cook dinner.

27

He went all out on Crazy Hair Day, and didn't cheer too loudly at the school play.

He makes up funny bedtime stories, and carries us to bed even when he knows we're not really asleep.

Hmmm…

Now that I think about it, he's actually pretty awesome.

Not bad, Dad!